"For I know the plans I have for you,"
declares the LORD, *"plans to prosper*
you and not to harm you, plans to
give you hope and a future."

— Jeremiah 29:11

Books may be purchased in quantity and/or special sales by contacting the
publisher, Bible Belles, at hello@biblebelles.com.

Published in San Diego, California, by Bible Belles. Bible Belles is a
registered trademark.

This book was created as a result of hard work, prayers, coffee, prayers, a
lot of late nights, prayers, so much help from others, prayers, and a whole
bunch of God's grace. Did we mention prayers?

Illustrations by: Megan Crisp and Rob Corley

Interior Design by: Ron Eddy

Cover Design by: Rob Corley and Ron Eddy

Editing by: Julie Breihan

Printed in the United States

ISBN 978-0-9961689-6-0

The Adventures of Rooney Cruz

HEARD

A Devotional for Girls

written by
Erin Weidemann

illustrated by
Megan Crisp and Rob Corley

CONTENTS

Hi there! I'm so glad you're here.

If you're anything like me, you care deeply about the next generation of girls. You already know that the world is sending them a constant stream of messages that tell them to look hot, act rude, and be loud.

I believe with all my heart that God wants you and me to do something about it.

We are in a battle for our girls' identities, and fighting hard isn't going to matter unless we have the right weapons. As a complement to Bible Belles' The Adventures of Rooney Cruz book series, these devotions will take you and your girl on a journey to discover how five areas of spiritual growth can inspire her to live in the world and not be corrupted by it.

When we come alongside our girls to develop these five qualities of character, we will lead them to a place where they know their true value and are prepared to step boldly into God's plan and purpose for their lives.

It is an incredible honor to partner with you to raise up a generation of girls who put the "her" in hero.

Blessings,
Erin

Welcome, Little Belle.

Your superhero journey
begins right now…

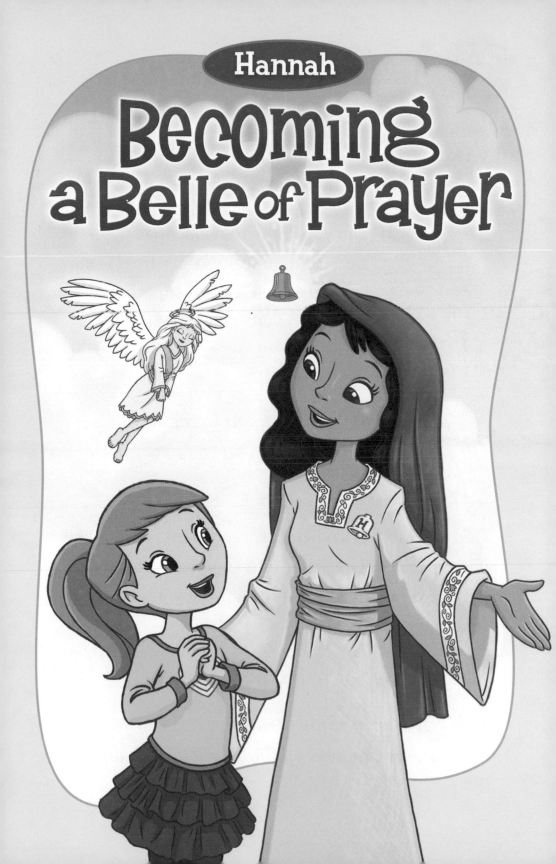

A REAL SUPERHERO

Welcome, Little Belle! You're about to find out a secret that not many people know. Are you ready?

Did you know that God made you to be a REAL superhero? It's true! It may be hard to believe, but superheroes are real. And YOU are one of them.

Jeremiah 1:5

Before I formed you in the womb I knew you, before you were born I set you apart.

God went to work when He created you. He made you with special gifts, talents, and superhuman abilities. No one is exactly like you! God made you special: a real superhero!

Psalm 139:13–16 NASB

For You formed my inward parts; You wove me in my mother's womb. I will give thanks to

You, for I am fearfully and wonderfully made; wonderful are Your works, and my soul knows it very well. My frame was not hidden from You, when I was made in secret, and skillfully wrought in the depths of the earth; your eyes have seen my unformed substance; and in Your book were all written the days that were ordained for me, when as yet there was not one of them.

And unlike other superheroes, you don't have to hide your powers from the rest of the world. Your identity is not a secret. You have special powers given to you by God, and you can use them any time you need them.

Activity: Discussion

Belle means "beautiful," and that's what YOU are. Ask your mom or dad what's beautiful about you. What are your special gifts? Tell them what you like about yourself. What are the things about you that are really beautiful, special, and unique?

THE POWER OF PRAYER

There are five main superpowers of the Bible Belles:
Prayer, Patience, Bravery, Loyalty, and Leadership.
Today you're going to find out how you can use your
first superpower: the Power of Prayer. We can see
how prayer is a power when we look at the story of
Hannah in I Samuel.

Read 1 Samuel 1:1–20.

Hannah was treated harshly by Peninnah. It would have been very easy for Hannah to shut down, get angry, or try to handle the problem herself. Instead, she brought her feelings to God in prayer and told Him the truth from inside her own heart.

And just as God heard Hannah's prayer, He hears yours too. Every single one.

Maybe you never thought that much about it before. Think about it right now. You have the ability to talk to God, and God can hear everything you say. God, the Creator of the entire universe, stops what He's doing and listens to you when you talk to Him. Amazing!

Activity: Memory Verse

Isaiah 45:3

I will give you hidden treasures, riches stored in secret places, so that you may know that I am Lord, the God of Israel, who calls you by name.

USE YOUR SUPERPOWER! TALK TO GOD

God wants to be close to you, and He's waiting for you to come and talk to Him. It's easy to get distracted, especially if you're feeling sad, angry, or frustrated.

James 4:8 NASB

Draw near to God and he will draw near to you.

It's also easy to forget about Him when you're happy or when things are going really well. To get close to God, you have to talk to Him as often as you can. That can be tough, though, because we can't see Him.

Psalm 145:18

The Lord is near to all who call on him, to all who call on him in truth.

Think of it like this: When you want to pray, imagine God is standing on the other side of a closed window. If you want Him to hear you, you have to open it. No matter what situation you find yourself in, it's easy. Just open the window and tell him what's on your mind.

Hebrews 4:16

Let us then approach God's throne of grace with confidence, so that we may receive mercy and find grace to help us in our time of need.

Activity: Drawing

Draw a picture using today's verse from Hebrews as inspiration: God on the "throne of grace" and you walking toward Him. Color it and hang it in your room as a reminder of how you get closer to God when you pray to Him.

DAY 4

OPEN THE WINDOW AND T-A-P: THANK HIM

Psalm 95:2

Let us come before him with thanksgiving and extol him with music and song.

Remember, you can think of prayer like you're opening a window. When it's open, God is there on the other side, waiting to hear from you. Then, just remember to tap the window (T-A-P) and tell Him what's on your mind.

1 Chronicles 16:34

Give thanks to the Lord, for he is good; his love endures forever.

The "T" in TAP stands for "Thank." God has given us many gifts, wonderful people, and special blessings. He has given us a beautiful world to live in, and He takes care of our every need. Be sure to tell Him how happy and grateful you are for His love, protection, and grace. Thank Him for everything you can think of!

Craft: Prayer Window

Make your very own prayer window! Create one from scratch by decorating a cardboard cutout, or use one made of real wood that's been repurposed. Paint it, decoupage it, bedazzle it. Be creative! Add pictures and words to remind you of reasons you want to say "thank You" to God.

DAY 5 — OPEN THE WINDOW AND T-A-P: ASK HIM

1 Samuel 1:27

I prayed for this child, and the Lord has granted me what I asked of him.

Hannah was a faithful and devoted servant, and God heard her prayer. He loved Hannah, just like He loves you, and that love allows us to be open and honest with Him about how we are feeling.

God's plan for Hannah was a special one, and it required her to be Samuel's mom. God has a special plan for you too, Little Belle!

1 John 5:14

This is the confidence we have in approaching God: that if we ask anything according to his will, he hears us.

The "A" in TAP stands for "Ask." God has the answer to every single question you have. No matter if you are feeling sad, lonely, confused, or angry, you can ask Him anything. He is always listening, and He wants you to ask Him your questions.

Activity: Make a List

Create a list today of things you want to ask God about. You can color code each entry for different feelings (for example, red for anything that's making you angry, green for happy, and so on). Did you make a mistake? Ask God for forgiveness. Are you feeling confused about something? Ask God to help you understand. Are you angry with a friend or feeling left out? Ask God for some advice. Is someone you know sick? Ask God to help them feel better. Are there people you know who are having trouble? Ask God to protect them and help them through it.

Add these thoughts and ideas to your prayer window. They will remind you that you can always ask God for anything: forgiveness, information, help, advice, healing, protection . . . even a miracle!

OPEN THE WINDOW AND T-A-P: PRAISE HIM

God answered Hannah's prayer by giving her a son: Samuel!

Read "Hannah's Prayer" in 1 Samuel 2:1–10.

Samuel means "God heard." Hannah lifted up her voice to declare that God was with her. He heard her prayer. God is strong and mighty! He has the power to do great and wonderful things in your life too. He made you a superhero, after all!

Psalm 86:12

I will praise you, Lord my God, with all my heart; I will glorify your name forever.

The "P" in TAP stands for "Praise." God made this entire world and everything in it (Psalm 89:11): everything we can see, touch, hear, smell, and taste. He is awesome and mighty and powerful, so celebrate and tell Him so! You can be happy and excited that God is who He is. He is loving, faithful, and worthy of our praise.

Activity: Word Search

Find Psalm 145 in your Bible and read it aloud. Write down a few verses or some words and phrases that you like. Add them to your prayer window as a reminder to praise Him always.

LIKE HANNAH, YOU ARE A BELLE OF PRAYER!

You did it! You've earned your first bell: the Bell of Prayer. It's yours to keep. It will remind you of the power you have to talk to God and tell Him the truth, just like Hannah. Remember, God can hear you, and He is always listening.

1 Thessalonians 5:17–18 NASB

Pray without ceasing; in everything give thanks.

This power is yours to use whenever you need it. Forever. So take good care of it. Protect it and use it as often as you can. That's how it will grow to be really strong!

Colossians 4:2

Devote yourselves to prayer, being watchful and thankful.

Activity: Share a Prayer

Today share your Bell of Prayer with someone else! Draw a bell like the one you see on the previous page, and add your favorite verse about prayer. Now share it with a friend who could use the Power of Prayer in her life!

NOTES

DAY 1 *YOU ARE GOD'S MASTERPIECE*

Welcome back, Little Belle! Your superhero journey continues right now.

Colossians 1:16

For by Him all things were created, both in the heavens and on earth, visible and invisible.

Even before you were born, God knew exactly who He wanted you to be. God didn't just create you quickly. Like all of creation, He took His time. God carefully planned every detail of you, and He made you special, unique, and beautiful. There is no one exactly like you, and God has a very special plan and purpose for your life.

Ephesians 2:10

For we are God's handiwork, created in Christ Jesus to do good works, which God prepared in advance for us to do.

Activity: Prayer

Dear God,

Thank You for making me a masterpiece! You carefully planned out everything about me. That is awesome! Please help me remember that You created me for a very special plan. There are "good works" You want me to do that no one else can do. Please help me find out what they are and give me the strength to do them. Please guide me. I want to become the beautiful hero You created me to be. Amen.

THE POWER OF PATIENCE

Remember, there are five main superpowers of the Bible Belles: Prayer, Patience, Bravery, Loyalty, and Leadership. Today you're going to find out how you can use your second superpower: the Power of Patience. We can see how patience is a superpower when we look at the story of Esther.

After Esther became the queen of Persia (Esther 2), her cousin Mordecai got into some trouble by refusing to bow to Haman, the king's second in command (Esther 3). Haman became very angry and came up with a plan to destroy all of God's people.

Read Esther 4.

When her people were threatened, Esther faced a difficult choice. It would have been very easy for her to hurry to talk to the king without thinking it through. Instead, Esther took her time. She prepared her heart by praying and fasting. She waited and listened for God to guide and direct her.

And just as God helped Esther to wait patiently until it was the right time to act, He will help you too.

Activity: Memory Verse

Psalm 130:5

I wait for the Lord, my whole being waits, and in his word I put my hope.

BE STILL

Have you ever done something before really thinking it through? A lot of the time people don't pause or prepare their hearts before making a choice. They jump in before taking enough time to pray, think, or ask God for help.

Psalm 37:7

Be still before the Lord and wait patiently for him.

Having patience means taking time alone with God to allow Him to share something with us. Instead of rushing to make a decision too quickly, God says to be still. When we are still, sitting quietly and without anything there to distract us, it gives us a chance to hear what God wants to tell us.

Exodus 14:14

The Lord will fight for you; you need only to be still.

The Bible says that when we choose to wait on the Lord, taking time to properly prepare before making choices, He gives us the power and strength we need so that we can make the best choice at the right time.

Activity: Drawing

Draw a picture using today's verse from Exodus as inspiration: God fighting and you being quiet and still. Color it and hang it in your room as a reminder of how God is in charge and it's our job to wait for Him.

HIS TIMING IS PERFECT

Remember, sometimes it can be really hard to wait, especially if you are feeling angry, hurt, or frustrated. But God's plans are perfect, and that includes His timing for when things will happen.

Psalm 62:5

My soul, find rest in God; my hope comes from him.

You have the power to control yourself: to slow down, pause, sit quietly, and prepare your heart to wait for whatever God has planned. All you have to do is trust Him.

Hosea 12:6

Return to your God; maintain love and justice, and wait for your God always.

Craft: Patience Clock

Make your very own patience clock. Create one from scratch by decorating a cardboard cutout, or build one out of materials you have at home. Paint it, decorate it, dress it up . . . Be creative! Add pictures and words that will help you to remember to "wait on the Lord" and that His timing is perfect.

FOR SUCH A TIME AS THIS

Read Esther 4:1–14.

Esther was a little nervous to take on such a big responsibility, but Mordecai knew in his heart that she was in the palace for a very special purpose. Their people were in danger, and God's plan required Esther to make a tough decision. So what did she do?

Read Esther 4:15–16 and Esther 5:1–8.

Instead of acting quickly, Esther chose to spend time with God. She prayed for three days and waited for just the right time to approach the king. She came to him carefully, and with respect, inviting him to a banquet she had prepared. This was a gracious and considerate gesture, and it pleased the king. He was willing to listen to her.

Activity: Quick Write

Read Psalm 25:4–5 aloud a few times. Write down 4 to 5 words or phrases that stick out to you (Some ideas: "your ways," "guide me," "my hope is in you,"

and so on). Then add these words to your patience clock to remind you to always be looking and waiting for God's plan, His purpose, and His timing.

PRAISE HIM WHILE YOU WAIT

Read Esther 7:1–6.

Esther was able to save her people because she was prepared and ready to act at the right time. Esther was willing to wait, allowing God to guide her, and she was properly prepared for the right time to approach the king.

2 Samuel 22:31

As for God, his way is perfect: The Lord's word is flawless; he shields all who take refuge in him.

God knows and has planned every detail of our lives, and His plan is perfect. Because of this, we can trust Him. And when you trust God, you are choosing to live the life He created for you.

Psalm 71:14

As for me, I will always have hope; I will praise you more and more.

Activity: Song

What's your favorite song that you sing about God? Sing it now! Add some music notes, instruments, and some of your favorite lyrics to your patience clock to remind you to praise Him while you're waiting patiently.

LIKE ESTHER, YOU ARE A BELLE OF PATIENCE!

Way to go! You have officially
earned your second bell:
the Bell of Patience. This
bell is a symbol of the
power you have to wait
patiently for God's timing.
You can be still. You can
control yourself and how you
react to any situation you encounter,
just like Esther.

Isaiah 40:31

*But those who hope in the Lord
will renew their strength.
They will soar on wings like eagles;
they will run and not grow weary,
they will walk and not be faint.*

Remember, these powers, Prayer and Patience, are
God's gift to you. He wants you to use them as often
as you can.

Activity: Word Search

Find 1 Thessalonians 5:14 in your Bible. Read the verse aloud. On a separate piece of paper, write out the last phrase in the verse.

Be patient with everyone.

Hang it in your room as a reminder of what the Bible says about patience. It is for everyone!

DAY 1 *YOU ARE SET APART*

Way to go, Little Belle. You are making great progress.

Read aloud the verse below:

Jeremiah 1:5

Before I formed you in the womb I knew you, before you were born I set you apart.

When God made you, He set you apart. That means He made you different from everyone else. And another thing: God made you beautiful. Remember, that's what the word *belle* means. It's easy to get confused, though, about real beauty when you're looking out into the world.

Let's take a look at what God says about real beauty.

1 Peter 3:3–4

Your beauty should not come from outward adornment, such as elaborate hairstyles and the wearing of gold jewelry or fine clothes. Rather, it should be that of your inner self, the unfading beauty of a gentle and quiet spirit, which is of great worth in God's sight.

God tells us that our outer appearance is not how He measures beauty. God says that a "gentle and quiet spirit" is beautiful, not the way we look on the outside. Sometimes as girls and women (even moms too!), it's very hard to remember that. Not to worry! He's given us special powers that will help to create that "gentle and quiet spirit" inside us that is so precious to Him.

Activity: Prayer

Dear God,
Thank You for making something really special when You created me. You made me unique and different from everyone else, and that is awesome! I know there will be times in my life when I will forget, times when I won't feel beautiful. Please help me remember what You say about real beauty. It's not about what people can see on the outside. It's not about how I look or the clothes I wear. It's about my heart. Please be with me as I learn to become the beautiful hero that You created me to be. Amen.

THE POWER OF BRAVERY

Today you are going to find out how you can use your third superpower: the Power of Bravery. We can see how bravery is a superpower when we look at the story of Abigail in 1 Samuel.

Read the story of Abigail in 1 Samuel 25.

Abigail was faced with a difficult and dangerous choice. It would have been very easy for her to ignore the problem or be too scared to do anything about it. Instead, Abigail remembered that God was with her. She thought about how to protect her family and show David respect and kindness at the same time. She considered everyone involved in the problem, and she chose to solve it with a warm heart and solid thinking.

And just as God made Abigail brave, He makes you brave too.

Romans 8:31

If God is for us, who can be against us?

Maybe you never thought that much about it before. Think about it right now. You have the ability to stand up and face what scares you, no matter what situation you  find yourself in. Even if you are really afraid, God is always with you! There is no fight too great, no problem too scary, that you and God can't handle together.

Activity: Memory Verse

1 Corinthians 16:13–14

Be on your guard; stand firm in the faith; be courageous; be strong. Do everything with love.

DAY 3

THE LIGHT SHINES IN THE DARKNESS

Have you ever been so scared or nervous that it was hard to do something? Did it feel like you were frozen or like time was standing still? Have you ever felt like you knew the right thing to do, but you couldn't do it because something was holding you back?

Read Psalm 27:1–3.

Bravery is a feeling of confidence and strength, even when you are faced with trouble or danger. During those times, it's easy to forget that God is bigger than our problems. That's why we need lots of reminders of exactly who God is.

John 1:5

The light shines in the darkness, and the darkness has not overcome it.

Game: Lights Out

Tonight, before bed, ask your mom or dad to get a flashlight and sit in your room with you. Spend a few moments together in the dark. How do you feel?

What do you notice?

After a few minutes, turn on your flashlight. Shine the light in different places around the room (preferably not in your eyes!). How do you feel when you get to turn on the light?

Every time you pointed the light somewhere in the room, the darkness went away. This is what God is: our light in the darkness. When He is there, the darkness goes away! Say a special prayer and thank God that, because of who He is, you don't have to be afraid. We can be brave because of who He is!

DO NOT FEAR

God wants you to feel strong and excited to make good choices, and He's waiting for you to trust Him. It's easy to become afraid or nervous, though, especially if you come up against a situation that makes you feel uncomfortable or scared.

For example, if a group of girls is treating someone unfairly, it's easy to go along with the crowd. It's a lot harder to defend the one person being mistreated, but that's exactly the kind of thing that God wants to help you do. A lot of the time, though, the right choice is the most difficult one.

Isaiah 41:10

So do not fear, for I am with you; do not be
dismayed, for I am your God.
I will strengthen you and help you; I will uphold
you with my righteous right hand.

When you need to be brave, God says, "Do not fear."
He is with you! Close your eyes and imagine that God
is standing right next to you. Even if it's hard for you
to know exactly what to do, you can trust that God
is there. You don't have to try and be strong all on
your own. He promises to make you strong, and He
promises to help you.

The "right hand" in Scripture symbolizes power and
strength, and God says that He will hold us up. We do
not have to do it by ourselves.

Activity: Drawing

Draw a picture using today's verse from Isaiah as
inspiration: you, shoulders back and head held high,
standing on God's "righteous right hand" while He
holds you up. Color it and hang it in your room as
a reminder of how God is the one who makes you
brave.

DAY 5

MY STRENGTH AND MY SHIELD

We've talked about how bravery is a confident and strong feeling, even when you're scared, but that's only half the battle. The rest of bravery comes when you trust God and choose to love others, no matter how you are treated. It's hard, but God will help you!

Psalm 28:7

The Lord is my strength and my shield; my heart trusts in him, and he helps me.
My heart leaps for joy, and with my song I praise him.

When you need God to help you be brave, remember that the Lord is your strength and your shield. He will help you to be strong. He will protect you and keep you safe. If you need help feeling His protection, use the letters of the word *shield* to remember what bravery looks and feels like.

42

Shoulders back

Head high

Imagine God right next to you

Eyes forward

Listen with an open heart

Decide how best to show love and kindness

Activity: Power Pose

Stand in front of a mirror. Plant your feet in an open, wide stance. Call out each of the elements of S.H.I.E.L.D. as you act them out. This activity will help your brain and body remember what it looks and feels like to be brave!

MY HEART LEAPS FOR JOY

Read yesterday's verse, Psalm 28:7, again. Think about the second half of the verse:

My heart leaps for joy, and with my song I praise him.

―――――――――― ❧ ――――――――――

When we remember that God is strong, powerful, and always there to protect us, we can be happy and excited! We raise our hands and sing songs to God to show Him that we know He's always got our back, no matter what.

Activity: Song

What's your favorite song that you sing about bravery? Listen to it now. Write down some of the lyrics you like best and add them to your drawing from Day 4.

LIKE ABIGAIL, YOU ARE A BELLE OF BRAVERY!

Nice work! You've earned your third bell: the Bell of Bravery. Remember, you have the power to face any problem with the confidence that God is with you. He will see you through it, just like Abigail.

Deuteronomy 31:8

The Lord himself goes before you and will be with you; he will never leave you nor forsake you. Do not be afraid; do not be discouraged.

God is always with you, and He will make you brave!

Hebrews 13:6

So we say with confidence, "The Lord is my helper; I will not be afraid."

Activity: Brave Belle Challenge

Do you remember your Power Pose and what the Bible says in Psalm 28:7?

The Lord is my strength and my _____ .

Practice the pose until you can remember the action that goes with each letter. If you need help, ask an adult to say the actions first so you can repeat them. You can use your Power Pose any time you feel afraid. Remember, God is your Protector!

NOTES

Ruth

Becoming a Belle of Loyalty

HE CALLS YOU BY NAME

Great job. You're almost there!

You've been learning that God gave you superpowers, real ones that you can use any time you need them. Check out the verse below.

Isaiah 45:3

I will give you hidden treasures, riches stored in secret places, so that you may know that I am the Lord, the God of Israel, who calls you by name.

Even before you were born, God knew exactly the kind of hero He wanted you to be. He carefully planned every detail of you. He took His time because He had a very special plan and purpose in mind.

John 15:16

You did not choose me, but I chose you and appointed you so that you might go and bear fruit

So, what are you waiting for? It's time for you to become who God created you to be!

Activity: Prayer

Dear God,

Thank You for making me a real superhero! Please help me remember that You created me for a special purpose. There are jobs that You want me to do that no one else can do. I want to discover what they are! Thank You for helping me look, listen, and search for the assignments You have that are just for me. I want to become the hero You made me to be. I know I can do it with Your help. Amen.

THE POWER OF LOYALTY

Today you will learn how to use your fourth superpower: the Power of Loyalty. We can see how loyalty is a superpower when we look at the story of Ruth.

Read her story in Ruth 1.

It would have been very easy for Ruth to let Naomi continue the journey home by herself. Instead, Ruth chose to stay with her. Naomi lost the people she loved most in the world: her husband and her sons. Ruth knew that Naomi needed someone to love her. She might have felt nervous or scared to leave her home, but she put Naomi's needs ahead of her own feelings.

That's exactly how God wants you to love people: faithfully. He created you to be loyal!

1 John 3:18

Dear children, let us not love with words or speech but with actions and in truth.

Ruth didn't just tell Naomi she loved her. She showed her love by staying by her side. As you learn to use this power, you'll notice that it's easy to say you love someone and a bit harder to actually show it. God gave you the ability to think through any situation you face and decide the best way to show love. You can love others, no matter how they're treating you or how you feel.

Activity: Memory Verse

Proverbs 17:17

A friend loves at all times.

LOVE AND FAITHFULNESS

Think back to the last time someone hurt your feelings. Maybe it was during an argument or a misunderstanding. How did you feel?

Loyalty is showing love and genuine kindness toward others, despite how you may be feeling. It means loving others faithfully, without waiting or wanting something in return. This is tough to do, especially when a friend hurts us or when someone is pushing us away. It can feel a lot easier to ignore the person or do something to hurt the person back.

But you are a hero, and part of God's plan for you is that you would love the people around you. Friends. Enemies. Everyone. No matter what.

Proverbs 3:3

Let love and faithfulness never leave you; bind them around your neck, write them on the tablet of your heart.

Sounds tough, doesn't it? Don't worry. God will help you! When you find yourself in a situation where it feels hard to love someone, you need to remember that God is love. He is the best place to go when you need help loving the people around you.

Activity: Drawing

Draw a picture using today's verse from Proverbs as inspiration: you, standing tall, with the words *love* and *faithfulness* tied around your neck. Be creative! Color it and hang it in your room as a reminder of how God wants you to love others faithfully. That's what loyalty is all about.

SERVE WITH ALL YOUR HEART

God wants you to use your power! He created you to love the people around you, and He wants to help you do it. It's easy to become discouraged, though. It's hard to love someone who you feel isn't loving you back, but that's exactly what God wants you to do. He wants you to remember how He loves people.

John 13:34

As I have loved you, so you must love one another.

God loves us, even though we make mistakes every single day. He forgives every bad thought, angry mood, and wrong choice. He gives us His grace, no questions asked.

Ephesians 6:7

Serve wholeheartedly, as if you were serving the Lord, not people.

We all have people in our life, and they all need love. The truth is that some people are easier to love than others. When you need to show love and kindness to someone, try to imagine that God is the one who needs it. How would you do things differently if He were the one standing in front of you?

Activity: A Big Heart

On a piece of paper, make two columns. Think about the people you know (family, friends, classmates, teammates). In the first column, make a list of people you think are easy to love. In other words, it wouldn't be difficult to be kind to these people. It would only take a little bit of effort and a little heart.

In the second column, make a list of people in your life who are a little harder to love. Once you have some names written down, spend some time thinking and praying out loud with your mom or dad. Ask God to change your heart for these people. Ask God to make your heart bigger for the people in the second column.

A CORD OF THREE STRANDS

We've talked about how loyalty is a choice. It's making the decision to love people faithfully, no matter what. We need God's help to do this, but we also need people: friends, family members, and others who love God and will stand with us to love and serve.

Ecclesiastes 4:9–12

Two are better than one,
*   because they have a good return*
*   for their labor:*
If either of them falls down,
*   one can help the other up.*
But pity anyone who falls
*   and has no one to help them up.*
Also, if two lie down together, they will keep warm.
*   But how can one keep warm alone?*
Though one may be overpowered,
*   two can defend themselves.*
A cord of three strands is not quickly broken.

God does not want you to try to love everyone around you all by yourself! He wants you to stand together with the people who love and care about you. That way, if you hit a stumbling block or become discouraged, someone will be there to pick you up.

Look back at your "Big Heart" lists from yesterday. Ask someone in the first column to help you choose one person from the second column that you want to serve. Brainstorm ways that the two of you can work together to show love to that person this week. Make it an act of service that you can start, continue, and finish together.

DAY 6 · *HIS GREAT LOVE*

Read today's verse.

John 15:13

Greater love has no one than this: to lay down one's life for one's friends.

Ruth shows us what it means to be loyal: to put another person's feelings ahead of our own. It makes sense that she is such a great example of true kindness and sacrifice. She became part of the lineage of Jesus: one of the best examples we have of love and loyalty!

Psalm 117:2

For great is his love toward us, and the faithfulness of the Lord endures forever. Praise the Lord.

Activity: Song

What's your favorite song that you sing about God's love? Sing it now! Add some music notes, instruments, and some of your favorite lyrics to your drawing from Day 3.

God's love is loyal. It will never change. He will never leave us, and that is a reason to celebrate!

LIKE RUTH, YOU ARE A BELLE OF LOYALTY!

You've earned it: your very own Bell of Loyalty. It's yours to keep. It will remind you of the power you have to love others faithfully, just like Ruth.

Psalm 86:15

But you, Lord, are a compassionate and gracious God, slow to anger, abounding in love and faithfulness.

Remember, God loves you, and with His help, you can love others too! This power is yours to use whenever you need it. Forever. Take good care of it. Protect it and use it as often as you can. That's how it will grow to be really strong!

Deuteronomy 7:9

Know therefore that the Lord your God is God; he is the faithful God, keeping his covenant of love to a thousand generations of those who love him and keep his commandments.

Activity: Bell of Loyalty

Today share your Bell of Loyalty with someone else! Draw a bell like the one you see here, and add your favorite verse about loyalty. Now share it with another little belle who could use the Power of Loyalty in her life!

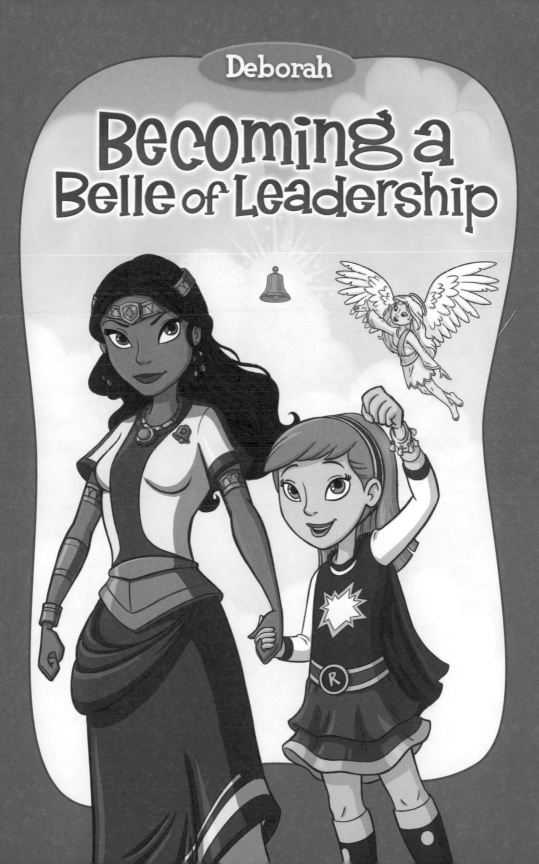

DAY 1 · CALLED TO LEAD

Excellent work, Little Belle. You're almost there!

Read the verse below.

Isaiah 64:8

Yet you, Lord, are our Father. We are the clay, you are the potter; we are all the work of your hand.

God worked to create you, and do you know what else? God has work for you to do. He gave you a powerful voice. He wants you to use the voice He gave you to change the world.

Psalm 100:1–3

Shout for joy to the Lord, all the earth.
Worship the Lord with gladness;
come before him with joyful songs.

Know that the Lord is God.
   It is he who made us, and we are his;
   we are his people, the sheep of his pasture.

Are you ready to be the leader God created you to be?

Activity: Prayer

Dear God,
You have called me to be a leader. Thank You! You created me with a voice unlike anyone else's, and You have important work for me to do. Please help me keep my eyes, ears, and heart open for ways that You want me to lead. Amen.

DAY 2 *THE POWER OF LEADERSHIP*

Today you're going to find out how you can use your fifth superpower: the Power of Leadership. We can see how leadership is a superpower when we look at the story of Deborah.

Read the story of Deborah in Judges 4.

Deborah was a woman who dedicated her life to serving others. As a judge, she helped people solve their disagreements. She gave them good advice and encouraged them to do the right things.

1 Peter 5:6

Humble yourselves, therefore, under God's mighty hand, that he may lift you up in due time.

Deborah was a humble servant, choosing to value God and people more than she valued herself. Because of her faith, strength, and character, God placed Deborah in a position to lead His people into battle and win a great victory!

And, just like God chose Deborah to be a leader, He chose you too.

Activity: Memory Verse

Philippians 2:3–4

Do nothing out of selfish ambition or vain conceit. Rather, in humility value others above yourselves, not looking to your own interests but each of you to the interests of the others.

DAY 3 *OVERCOME EVIL WITH GOOD*

When you think of a leader, what comes to mind? What do leaders actually do?

Romans 8:28

And we know that in all things God works for the good of those who love him, who have been called according to his purpose.

Deborah's story shows us that being a true leader is much more than simply being in charge of a group of people. It's about living the life God created you to live and being bold and confident to do the work He has for you to do.

Romans 12:21

Do not be overcome by evil, but overcome evil with good.

Remember, just like Rooney, God gave you superpowers. You can use these powers—prayer, patience, bravery, loyalty, and leadership—to overcome evil in the world. Just like a real superhero!

Activity: Drawing

Draw a picture using today's verse from Romans 12:21 as inspiration: you, dressed as a superhero, fighting against and defeating evil. Color it and hang it in your room as a reminder of how you are a bold leader for God!

DAY 4 *SPUR ONE ANOTHER*

Leadership is more than being in charge or telling people what to do. It doesn't only mean doing the work God wants you to do. Being a good leader also means encouraging the people around you to do the same.

Hebrews 10:24–25

And let us consider how we may spur one another on toward love and good deeds, not giving up meeting together, as some are in the habit of doing, but encouraging one another—and all the more as you see the Day approaching.

God created you to show His love to others. He also created you to help other people to love and serve too. We do this by inspiring those around us and stirring them to action.

Activity: Adult-Child Discussion

Look up the word *encouragement* in the dictionary. Spend some time talking about the definition.

This word literally means to "put courage in" others.

Talk about a time you were struggling and someone encouraged you.

Discuss the following:

What were you facing?

What did the person say?

What did the person do?

How did it make you feel?

Pray together and ask God to grow your desire and skill to encourage others in both words and actions.

HUMILITY AND WISDOM

Deborah gives us a great example of real leadership. It was her job to encourage the people around her. She placed her trust in the Lord and rose in confidence to lead her people to a great victory!

James 3:13

Who is wise and understanding among you? Let them show it by their good life, by deeds done in the humility that comes from wisdom.

Activity: Discussion

Read Deborah's song in Judges 5 and discuss the following questions.

1. *Why do you think Deborah is called "a mother in Israel" (v. 7)?*

2. *Read Judges 5:10–12 again. Why do you think verse 12 calls for Deborah to "wake up" and "break out in song"?*

It's time to put it all together. God wants you to use your powers!

Hannah

Prayer

Esther

Patience

Abigail

Bravery

Ruth

Loyalty

Deborah

Leadership

Craft: Charm Bracelet

Make your very own HEARD bracelet with yarn, string, cord, craft foam, or whatever other fun material you prefer. Be creative! Use beads, jewels, charms, letters, and more!

Be sure to add the initials of each Bible Belle ("H" for Hannah, "E" for Esther, "A" for Abigail, "R" for Ruth, and "D" for Deborah). Wear your HEARD bracelet as a reminder that, like the Bible Belles, God gave YOU a powerful voice. He wants that voice to be heard out in the world!

DAY 7
LIKE DEBORAH, YOU ARE A BELLE OF LEADERSHIP!

You did it! You've earned your fifth bell: the Bell of Leadership. It will remind you of the power you have to be a bold leader, just like Deborah.

Psalm 48:14

For this God is our God for ever and ever; he will be our guide even to the end.

Remember, God is your leader. He is always with you, and He will help you be the leader He created you to be!

Isaiah 30:21

Whether you turn to the right or to the left, your ears will hear a voice behind you, saying, "This is the way; walk in it."

Activity: Prayer

Thank You, God, for calling me to be a leader. Help me grow in strength and confidence to do the work You want me to do. As I walk through life with You by my side, please help me remember to follow You. You are my leader! Amen.

For games, activities, and more, visit **biblebelles.com**